Anne Rooney does not eat meat, in case the taste of blood becomes too appealing.

When not writing books she haunts the cemeteries and catacombs of Paris and Venice and raises non-vampiric daughters and chickens in Cambridge. She studied at a haunted college and her first car was a haunted van; the undead hold no fears for her.

With thanks to Kate, Hannah and Sue Frew, Mary
Hoffman and Shahrukh Husain.

In Cold Blood

by Anne Rooney
www.annerooney.co.uk

Published by Ransom Publishing Ltd.
Radley House, 8 St. Cross Road, Winchester, Hants.
SO23 9HX, UK
www.ransom.co.uk

ISBN   978 184167 160 4

First published in 2012

A CIP catalogue record of this book is available from the British Library.

Vampire
Dawn

Die Now
or
Live Forever

ANNE ROONEY

Ransom

One

It's not what you expect to see, a corpse nailed to the ground with a tent peg. Finn saw it first.

'What the ... There's some right nutter around here.'

He clenched his fists as he did whenever he felt a fight coming on.

Omar stumbled into him.

'Whaaat!' he cried out, feeling his stomach rise. Juliette was just a step behind. She said nothing, simply raised both hands to cover her mouth. Ruby was helping Alistair untangle a bramble that had caught his T-shirt.

'What's up?' she called.

'There's a dead guy here.'

'What?' she pushed forward, no longer noticing the brambles snatching at her legs. Alistair trailed behind her with his head down, looking at his feet.

Omar's first instinct was to run. But instead he heaved his backpack onto the ground, the clatter of the tent pegs in it suddenly threatening. He'd never seen a dead person before. He was afraid and disgusted, but also curious – and ashamed to feel curious.

'Better see if he's still alive,' he said.

But he knew the guy wasn't alive. He was very pale, greyish, and as soon as Omar touched the skin, its cold firmness told him that they were too late. There was blood soaking through the T-shirt around the tent peg. It didn't look as though the tent peg should have been enough to kill someone – it was so thin, so ordinary.

'Why on earth did he lie still for someone to nail a tent peg through his chest?' asked Finn. It was a fair question.

'Perhaps he was unconscious,' Omar suggested. 'Or drunk.' He leant over the body and sniffed, but couldn't smell alcohol.

'Are you seriously sniffing a corpse?'

'We should call the police,' said Ruby, coming alongside them and running her hands through her spiky hair, brown prickles sticking out between her chunky rings.

'Yeah, right. That'll be easy. You know the Hungarian for 'there's a dead guy with a tent peg through his chest', do you? Is it in your phrasebook?'

'Well, what *should* we do? We can't just leave him here.' It was the first time Juliette had spoken.

'Yes we can. That's *exactly* what we can do. We don't know what crazy did this. We don't know if he's still around. We have two bags of tent pegs, we don't speak the language and we don't have an alibi. We're better off pretending we haven't seen it. We don't want to get the blame.' Finn hoisted his backpack and turned back towards the path.

'But that's terrible! We can't!' Omar said.

'It doesn't matter whether it's terrible,' said Finn. 'Haven't you seen enough CSI episodes? Did you touch him? There'll be some of your DNA on him. Let's get out of here.'

But no one moved. It didn't seem possible, somehow, just to walk back into the forest, knowing there was a dead body there. Not just a dead body – a murdered body.

Because a murdered body meant a murderer, and camping in a scary forest was one thing, but camping in a forest where you know there's a murderer walking around – well, it's a different thing altogether. Not even just a normal, run-of-the-mill murderer who might shoot you or something. But a complete freak, who would nail you to the forest floor while you screamed and flailed and bled, and he just kept on hammering away at the tent peg.

'Come on,' said Ruby eventually. 'Whatever we're going to do later, we're not hanging around near this. Let's go.' She turned and stalked purposefully towards the trees.

'Shhhh!' hissed Juliette. There was a noise. A rustling of leaves, the snap of a twig, then silence.

'Whoever it was, they're still here,' she whispered.

Each of them stood still, hearts beating unbearably fast. Only their eyes moved, scanning the edges of the forest, the short metres the light reached, looking for someone or something but finding nothing.

A crash of wings broke the silence as some bird

flapped into the sky. Ruby stopped breathing. But something else did not stop breathing. Shallow, fast breaths to her left. She didn't dare to turn her head, let *it* know she knew it was there. She signalled to Juliette with her eyes. *Please notice*, she willed her.

The bird rose high, then swooped over the distant lake. Juliette started walking towards Ruby and the others followed, but Ruby still didn't move, expecting at any moment that some madman would leap out at her. She wanted to run, but her legs took no notice. As Juliette drew alongside her, she touched her arm.

'You OK?'

Ruby shook her head and pointed to where the breathing came from.

Juliette signalled to the others. They all moved towards the tangle of bushes, hearts pounding. A shape – small, slender – went crashing through the undergrowth as they approached, blonde hair flying out behind and catching in the branches.

'It was a girl!' Ruby said in surprise. 'Did a girl murder him?'

'More likely she thinks we did,' said Finn. 'No point going after her – even if we catch her, she won't understand us.'

'Why do you think she's not the murderer?' asked Omar. 'Just because she's a girl? Girls can kill people, too, you know.'

Juliette flinched. Omar pushed the bushes aside with his foot. A dropped tent peg glinted amongst the dead leaves.

Two

Alistair fumbled with his phone, panic making his fingers clumsy.

'There's no signal. There's no signal here! What are we going to do? How will we know where to go?' His voice rose as though he would cry, but for once no one laughed at him. They all felt the same.

'We'll have to camp somewhere around here,'

Omar said. 'It's taken hours to get here – there's no way we can get anywhere tonight. We have a map – we don't need GPS.'

'I'm not camping near a dead guy!' Alistair was visibly trembling. Finn curled his lip in disgust.

'Not here, goon. We can walk on for a while. We'll go to the lake. It's only about an hour away. Then we can pitch our tents with the water behind us and no one can creep up on us. Backs to the wall. Old trick. Tomorrow we'll give up and get back to civilisation. We'll be OK tonight if we stick together. We can take it in turns to stay awake.'

'What about the mad axe-woman?' said Juliette.

'She hasn't got an axe, she's got tent pegs. There

are five of us – we're more than a match for a skinny kid with a bunch of tent pegs,' Ruby said.

It seemed to take years to get to the lake. Every snapped twig, every rustle in the bushes, every animal running or snuffling made their skin prickle.

At last, they pitched their two tents side by side on the shore of the lake. With the water behind them and some space before the trees, it looked safe enough. They lit a fire, cooked and tried to act as though everything was normal. But it wasn't. Life isn't normal if you're in the middle of a forest with only two other people, one of them dead and the other their killer.

'We should put out the fire – the light will make mosquitoes come,' said Alistair.

Omar and Juliette snuggled closer to it, leaning into each other. No one wanted it to be dark.

'I can't help thinking about that boy,' said Juliette. 'To die like that, with no warning. He must have thought he had forever.'

'Not forever,' said Omar, 'but maybe seventy years or so.'

'What would you choose,' mused Juliette, 'if you could die now or live forever? I mean, truly forever?'

'Live forever,' Omar answered. 'No brainer.'

'Die now,' said Ruby. 'If you truly lived forever, you'd still be here when there were no more people, when the Earth was frazzled up by the Sun or blasted to bits by a huge meteorite.'

'It wouldn't work, would it?' added Finn. 'You couldn't just be whizzing around in space with no air and no food. It's a stupid question.' Ruby took no notice, but gazed out over the lake.

'It's beautiful,' she said. 'We never see the Milky Way at home – there's too much light from all the buildings.'

Finn started to kick dirt onto the fire, swatting at a mosquito on his arm as he did so.

'Don't put it out,' pleaded Juliette. 'I'd rather have the mosquitoes than the tent-peg killer.'

'How many stars are there, Alistair?' Finn grinned cruelly as he said it.

'Shut up, Finn. Leave him alone.' Ruby was cross: it wasn't fair. But it was too late – Alistair was already trying to count the stars in the Milky Way.

She put a hand on his shoulder. 'Close your eyes. Count how many times I tap your arm instead.' He knew the trick. It was hard to close his eyes, but he did it and Ruby tapped away – 23, 24, 25, 26, 27, 28, 29. 29. It was always a prime number. He waited to see if she would go on to 31, but she didn't.

'29!'

'Time for bed,' she said, squeezing his hand, and he dipped into the tent.

'Why did you bring that freak?' Finn asked. 'Does he have OCD or something?'

'Yeah, something like that,' she said. 'He's not a

freak. What does it matter if he needs to count things? It doesn't harm you.'

'He's a baby.' Finn put his thumb in his mouth.

'It doesn't matter,' said Omar. 'Better someone who counts things than someone – '

'Stop it!' snapped Ruby. 'This is bad enough already without fighting. We didn't choose to be together, but we are. Let's focus on being safe and then getting out of here. Alistair's no trouble. And I'm looking after him, not you, so you can both shut up.'

'There are too many mozzies here,' said Omar. A slapping sound came from inside the tent. 'You got them in there, too, Alistair?' he called.

Alistair opened the flap.

'Yes. Look, I killed this one.'

'Good lad. Kill them all.'

'But look at it.' Alistair held out his hand with a squashed mosquito smeared across the palm. A smudge of red showed it had already bitten one of them.

'Nice. Well done. You can wipe it off now,' Omar said.

'No,' Alistair persisted. 'Look at it. It's not a normal mosquito. It's a different type.'

'It doesn't matter, Alistair,' Ruby said. 'Let's all see how many we can kill in our tents and then go to sleep.'

Alistair smiled. 'I'm going to keep it. I'm going to put it in my notebook.'

'Lovely,' muttered Finn. 'A collection of squashed mosquitoes. And you say he's not a freak?' He kicked dirt over the last of the fire and they huddled into their tents.

* * * * *

Outside, the forest crackled with night noises. Wolves howled in the distance. Closer to, a bag dropped onto dry leaves with a thud. No one heard it.

Three

Ruby was the first to wake.

'Ugh, mosquitoes! I'm covered in bites.' She
squinted in the sunlight. 'Why's it so bright today?
It hurts my eyes.'

'There are always mosquitoes near water – you
should know that,' Finn called from inside the
tent. 'Man up, girl!'

Soon they were all outside, scratching at their

bites and shading their eyes. Ruby slapped her arm and scratched hard, drawing blood. Apart from Alistair, who was arranging sticks at exact right-angles, they turned to stare at her.

'What? Stop staring, you're creeping me out.' She lifted her arm to her mouth and sucked the blood away.

Finn parted his lips.

'Shall I do that for you?'

'Are you coming onto me or something? That's just freaky. Leave me alone.'

'Breakfast anyone?' she asked, trying to break the awkward silence.

'Do we have any meat?'

As soon as Alistair asked, Ruby realised she wanted meat, too. But they didn't have any.

'Maybe we could catch something?' he suggested.

She was about to say this was stupid, but why shouldn't they catch something? After all, this was supposed to be an outdoor challenge trip. Why not catch rabbits or something for breakfast?

'Hey, math-boy,' yelled Finn. 'There are ants over here – why don't you come and count them? Or eat them.'

'Leave him alone!' snapped Ruby.

'What – are you his minder?' Finn turned on her.

'Yes, actually. He's my brother.'

Finn made an 'L for loser' sign at her. Ruby

raised her arm to hit him but stopped dead. There was a face peering out of the trees at them – the same face she'd seen near the dead camper.

The girl walked out and stood on the shore in front of them. She was skinny and grubby, with bits of leaf stuck in her hair and scratches on her bare legs.

For a long time no one spoke, but she looked at Ruby and they all looked at the rubber mallet in her hand. It was the type of mallet you use for bashing in tent pegs. Ruby spoke first.

'Do you speak English?'

The girl nodded. 'I'm Australian.'

Finn had his hand in his pocket, opening his penknife. Surely this skinny girl wasn't going to take on all five of them with a rubber mallet? He at least would put up a fight.

'What happened back there?' Ruby was going straight for it – Finn was impressed.

'He was my boyfriend.'

'Wouldn't want you as my girlfriend, then,' Omar said.

'He tried to kill me.'

'And you just happened to get him to lie down while you hammered a tent peg through his chest? That all sounds a bit *Chicago* to me – you know, 'he ran into my knife ten times'.'

The girl gave Omar a puzzled look. Perhaps she hadn't seen *Chicago*.

'He told me to take my crucifix off,' the girl said. A large, ugly crucifix hung around her neck.

'And he tried to bite me.'

'To *bite* you? What, like a vampire?' Finn raised his hands like claws, bared his teeth, hissed. And the girl stepped backwards.

'Yes. Like a vampire. Don't do that.'

'Haaach,' Finn threatened, leaning towards her. The girl raised her mallet.

'Finn, don't!' Ruby grabbed his arm. 'Calm down, everyone. I'm Ruby – this jerk is Finn. Stay where you are and tell us what happened.'

The girl pushed matted blonde hair away from her face, but it fell straight back.

'I'm Ava. He was Nathan. We're doing Europe for a year, been together for two. I thought I knew him inside out. And suddenly he acts like he wants to kill me. He acts like ... No, it's stupid.'

'Like what?' Finn had crouched down in front of her and was using his knife to cut blades of grass. He wanted her to see it.

'I don't know. Like someone completely different. Like some*thing* completely different.'

'Like a vampire?' Finn grinned, leaning across to drop the cut bits of grass in front of Alistair, silently inviting him to count them.

Ava looked at the ground and said nothing.

'So – ' Finn continued, 'he tried to bite you and you somehow held down this huge guy, despite your being, frankly, scrawny, and he stayed still while you nailed a tent peg through his chest? Not being funny, but you don't look the type. And I can't see him just lying there doing nothing – like 'Oh yeah, darling, just nail me to the floor'. Ah, was that it? Some creepy, weird game gone wrong?'

'No! He tried to bite me, but when he got close to my neck he sort of hissed and backed away. I've never seen him behave like that. I thought he was messing about at first, that it was a joke. But then he grabbed my wrist and I looked into his eyes and … and it was like he wasn't there. Not him, not the Nathan I know.'

'And so you nailed him to the floor? Bit harsh, no?'

'Finn, stop it! Let her speak.' Ruby waved her hands at him in a strange, fluttery gesture.

'He got ill. He lunged at me, I swung a fist at him. He fell back and swore at me. And he suddenly got ill again. He went pale, then threw up. He was shaking, convulsing, and all the time trying to grab at me, bite, scratch me. He was yelling that he would get me, that he would leave me just a shell, nothing. He was so strong. I couldn't fight him off, even when sick. I grabbed the mallet and then he ... he collapsed, still swearing he would get me. I was terrified.'

'And you nailed him to the floor when he passed out?'

'Yes.' It was barely a whisper.

'I was so scared. He said he'd get me. I didn't

know what to do. Where could I run? I was just so scared. I'm still scared.'

Finn was on his feet, jumping around, waving his knife, sandy hair spiking up around his head and his wiry limbs moving like the sails of a windmill, wildly.

'You are a total freaking nutter! You killed a guy who'd passed out? Why didn't you just run away? Or tie him up? Or ... or hurt him a bit? Are you crazy? ... You are! That's what you are! You're *crazy*! Crazy tent-peg girl.'

Alistair looked curiously at Finn's antics and started to smile. Ruby put a warning hand on his arm.

'You said he got ill again,' Omar said. 'So he'd already been ill?'

'Yes. I think he ate something bad. He's a bit of a bush-tucker freak.'

'A what?'

'In the outback, at home, he likes to go out and catch things and cook them. Lots of the guys do it. He did it here, I think, but we don't know what you can eat here and what you can't. So I guess he ate something that was bad somehow.'

'What, like magic mushrooms?' Omar suggested.

'I don't know. I don't know what he ate. Maybe. What do they do?'

'Well, they can make you sick and they can make you act crazy, and see things that aren't there, or think things that aren't true. But it would have worn off. If he weren't dead.'

Ava began to sob and shake.

'I killed him! I love him and I killed him. What am I going to do? What *can* I do? Oh please God, don't let this be real. Please, don't let him be dead.'

'So why on earth did you nail him?'

'Finn, stop it!' shouted Ruby. He raised his knife at her.

'Yeah? Why should I? She's a nutter. Crazy, tent-peg-killer nutter.'

four

Ruby felt faint. She put a hand to her head, which ached, and found it sweaty and hot, though she felt cold.

'I think I need to eat something,' she said. 'I'm feeling a bit weak.'

'Me too,' said Omar. 'What have we got?'

'Tinned beans, bread, apples, cheese, biscuits, tinned tuna, salted peanuts, cereal bars.'

'Do we have any more tinned sausages?' asked Alistair. 'I feel ill. I want sausages.'

'No, we don't – you've eaten them all.' Ruby realised she would prefer sausages, too, even though they were horrid.

Ava's eyes flickered over them all; Finn still held his knife, ready. She looked at the food Ruby had spilled out of the bag and that no one wanted to eat.

'Want some?' asked Omar. She nodded. He tore off some bread and passed it to her, broke off a piece of cheese, and tossed her a bottle of water. They all watched her eat.

At last, Alistair chewed a bit of bread himself. He didn't eat much. The others picked at cheese, biscuits and nuts, nibbling, not really wanting it.

'Aren't you lot hungry?' asked Ava. Her voice was anxious. That annoyed Finn. What did it matter to her if they ate or not?

'No. Shut up and eat if you want to.'

Behind him, Alistair was sick onto the grass. Ava gasped.

'Wassup? Not seen a kid puke before?'

She said nothing.

'Finn,' called Ruby. 'I don't feel well either.'

Ava blanched. 'It's ... it's what happened to Nathan. And then ... '

'And then you nailed him to the ground, as I recall,' said Finn. 'Well, you won't do that to us.'

He walked towards her, holding his knife out.

'No, I'll look after you,' she said quickly. 'He just went mad at me. I don't know why. It won't be like that.'

'How do we know that? You're a nutter. If we're sick and you still have your little packet of tent pegs ... No. Not happening.'

'Then what *is* happening?' asked Juliette. Ruby was already being violently sick.

'We'll tie her up,' said Omar. 'And when we're better, we'll take her with us and hand her over to the police. Fair, Ava?'

'NO! You can't tie me up! And you can't hand me over to the police. What will they do with me? This isn't even a civilised country.'

'Oh, I'm sure they'll be very interested to hear

that view. This is the EU: you'll get a fair trial. And, hey – you *did* kill him.'

While Omar was talking, Finn dodged round behind Ava. Now when she turned to run, he grabbed her and pulled her to the ground. Omar and Juliette were onto her in a moment.

'You're going nowhere!' shouted Finn, pulling her arms so far up behind her back that she screamed in pain.

Finn and Omar dragged Ava to a tree, ripped off their leather belts and strapped her to the trunk. Juliette unhitched a guy-rope from one of the tents – good, strong, nylon cord – and they tied her with that, too. Omar took Juliette's hair scrunchy and wound it round Ava's wrists behind the tree. All the time Ava screamed at them, then cried, pleaded and begged.

As soon as she was secure, Omar staggered away and threw up. Alistair had passed out, face down in the grass with vomit around him. Ruby dragged him onto his side, but that was all she could do.

Juliette touched Ruby's hair.

'I feel OK-ish. I'll try to find help, or at least get somewhere there's a phone signal. I'll be back. Don't worry.'

Omar pulled a map from his bag.

'Here. Take this. Mark where we are. Take my phone – it has a compass app. Be safe.'

Juliette stuffed the map and phone into her backpack, grabbed a bottle of water and pushed a

hand over her damp forehead. She picked up a
dropped sweater and set off along the beach.
Going round the lake seemed the best bet – there
was a car park a few kilometres further on.

Omar watched her go, then slumped down
with his back against a tree.

'What if you all die?' Ava screamed. 'What will
happen to me? I'll starve. You can't do this!'

Finn spat a mouthful of vomit onto the grass.

'We won't die. We're just a bit sick.'

'Nathan died.'

'He died because you nailed him to the floor!
And do you think we *care* what happens to you if
we die? Ha! Maybe you'll be eaten by wolves. Who
knows? Who cares? You freak!'

Finn was the last to pass out.

'No,' Ava whispered to no one, into the silent forest. 'No, he didn't.'

five

The hours dragged by. It was much colder at night than in the daytime. Ava shivered and struggled, but there was no way to work herself free. The belts cut into her ankles and her neck, and the nylon rope squeezed her waist and chest.

She had given up crying. There was no one to hear; just four bodies sprawled on the ground. She hoped there was no one to hear.

Just before sunrise, she heard something. Not only the sounds there had been all night – the owls that wailed like ghosts and the twigs snapping under the feet of goodness-knows-what. It was closer, repeated. Shuffling, and then a footstep. And another. The soft, muffled sound of footsteps over sand.

Ava froze. Not again.

'Alistair? Ruby? Are you OK?' It was Omar. Ruby groaned.

'I feel awful. What happened?' asked Ruby. She shook Alistair. 'Where's Finn?'

'Still out cold.' Omar bent over Finn's slumped shape. 'Oh God. He's not breathing!' His voice rose in panic.

'Does anyone know how to do that thing to start people's hearts and make them breathe?'

'CPR,' said Alistair. 'I still feel funny.' No one knew how to do it. Ruby noticed Ava – they'd forgotten her.

'Do you know it?' Ruby asked. Ava shook her head. She looked pale and terrified. Ruby squinted at her in the grey half-light.

'What are you so scared of? We aren't going to hurt you. We tied you up so that you didn't hurt us.'

'It happened to Nathan. Like this – like Finn.'

'What did? Nathan wasn't dead until you killed him. And if he *was* dead, you didn't need to nail him, did you?'

Behind her, Omar leaned on Finn's chest, trying to remember what he'd seen in a hundred episodes of *Emergency!* on TV.

'Be careful,' said Alistair, 'You might hurt him if you do it wrong.'

'He's dead, Alistair. I can't really hurt him any more than that, can I?'

'I'm not breathing, either.'

'What? Of course you're breathing. You can't talk without breathing.'

'Look. I'm not breathing like before.'

'Not now, Alistair. I've got to help Finn.'

Omar took his hands off Finn's chest, waited a moment, leaned on it again. What came next? Get some air into him, of course. That mouth-to-mouth thing. Eugh. He took a deep breath – and immediately his head was spinning. He felt as though he would explode. He let it out quickly. He tried again, a normal breath – and even that seemed strange.

'Alistair – what was that you said about breathing?'

'I don't breathe – or hardly. Look.'

'Are you holding your breath?'

'No! Test your own breathing.'

It was true; they were all taking very shallow breaths, barely noticeable.

'So maybe he's not dead,' said Omar at last.

'I have a funny taste in my mouth,' Alistair

said. 'And I really, really want some meat.'

'Not now,' said Ruby, helping Omar to revive Finn.

Finn's eyelids flickered, and soon he looked up at her. It only took a couple of minutes before he sat up, ran his fingers through his hair and said, 'Yeah, me too. Meat.'

They hunted again through their food bag, but there was nothing they wanted. Finn noticed Ava, shrinking back against the tree she was tied to, willing him not to see her. He looked at her, and something stirred in his stomach. He grinned – a nasty, threatening grin.

Omar sat back, now that Finn was clearly alive, and followed his gaze. His eyes settled on Ava.

He hadn't really looked at her before – not *really* looked. Now he saw her long, brown legs, streaked with dry blood that was so dark red it was almost brown. She had scratched them crawling through the brambles, but that didn't make them any less attractive. With her arms pulled back and tied behind her, behind the tree, her chest jutted out – even more so because the nylon cord around her body pulled her shirt tight against her. Her throat and chest were exposed between the leather belt and the unbuttoned shirt.

Omar couldn't take his eyes off her. At first she had looked away, but realising that wouldn't stop him staring at her, she now looked straight into his eyes. Involuntarily, he parted his lips. They were dry. He licked them once.

Her blue eyes held his gaze and her defiance challenged him. Or was it defiance? Perhaps she felt it too, this sudden, compelling attraction. He was irresistibly drawn to her.

He walked over to the tree, stopped just in front of her and looked for a long, long time. His eyes pulled to her bare, blood-smeared thighs again. He liked a girl who was active, not prissy about her clothes, had a spirit of adventure.

He looked at her face again, and into her eyes. There was something there he didn't recognise at first, but found deeply alluring. He wanted to remove the belt, to see her throat properly. He really wanted to do that, he realised. He looked back at her eyes and saw what it was. Fear.

A thrill ran though him. She was desperately

afraid of him but struggling not to show it. Her pupils were wide – so wide he felt sucked into them. He moved closer. He loved the rush it gave him that she was so scared, he didn't pause to think that this was not like him, not what he wanted to be at all. He moved closer and she grew more afraid. He would have to kiss her – he couldn't help himself. He would kiss her so hard she would bleed and he would carry on kissing her, so that the blood ran into his mouth, and …

Suddenly he had his hands on her shoulders and the others were at his side.

'What are you doing?' Finn, tried to push him, hard. Ruby looked confused. She was twisting her hands together and she, too, licked her lips. Why was this girl, scruffy and scared, suddenly so magnetic? Even Ruby couldn't look away from her.

Ava tried to face down Omar, but she couldn't cope with all of them.

Ava started to squirm and shout. As she struggled, the leather belt cut into her neck and a trickle of blood ran from under the buckle.

Omar put his finger to the blood and then raised it slowly, teasingly, to his lips. He felt his head explode with desire and pushed his mouth towards Ava's lips, even as she twisted away.

Six

'Stop!'

Omar froze. It wasn't Finn, or Alistair. It was a
deep, rich male voice. It took all of Omar's will
power to pull himself back from Ava's struggling
body and turn round. He was shaking and weak
with frustration.

They all turned at the same time. Two figures
were outlined against the sunlight glinting off the

lake. One was Juliette. The other, holding her hand, was a tall man, dressed in black. He had olive skin and was astonishingly handsome. He looked late-thirties, like a film star. His black hair was tousled, with only one or two streaks of grey. He looked totally relaxed, as though commanding the four of them was nothing to him and he had absolute confidence that they would obey him. And they did.

'What is happening here?'

His accent was mid-European, but there was something else to his voice, something quite hypnotic.

Omar didn't know what to say. He had no idea why the desire to kiss her had been so strong, why he'd needed to put his mouth to hers and taste her blood on his tongue – but even thinking about it made him want it again. He was ashamed, confused – and yet he wasn't. The feeling was stronger than shame; he didn't even care why he wanted to do it.

'We need her.' It was Finn.

'So I see.' The man folded his hands in front of him, as relaxed as could be. 'But you're not going to have her. Untie her.'

'But she'll escape,' said Finn. 'And she's a psycho killer. She – '

'I know. I've seen the boy. But she will neither run nor hurt you. Untie her.'

Omar watched Finn and Ruby remove the cord and the belts. He saw Ava reach up to rub her neck; two red lines ran across it. His longing to touch her, especially the wounds, was suffocating.

'Tell me why you attacked the boy,' the man said to Ava.

'He tried to kill me. He fell ill and then he went crazy and wanted to bite me. He got more ill and he died. I swear – he died.'

'Then why did you nail him to the floor?' shouted Finn.

'Because he came back! He started to get up again. He opened his eyes and looked into mine and I could see he still wanted to kill me. I was so terrified. The hammer was there beside him, and the tent pegs. It was all I had.

'I tried to stab him with a tent peg and he roared and reached out to grab me. I hit him over the head with the mallet, and then I hammered a peg tent through his chest. It was all I could do.

'He would have killed me, I swear he would. I can't believe I did it. I can't believe he wanted to kill me. We loved each other – we were so happy.' Crying took her over completely.

'Who bit him?' the stranger asked.

Ava did not appear to hear him, but carried on sobbing.

'Who bit all of you?'

They were confused.

'No one bit us,' said Finn. 'Why would anyone bite us?'

'You were going to bite *her* – weren't you?'

Omar realised he was. 'Yes.'

'So – you were bitten. Who by?'

'We weren't bitten by anyone,' said Alistair. 'Only by mosquitoes. They aren't an *anyone*, are they?'

'Mosquitoes?' The stranger seemed taken aback for the first time. 'That's impossible.'

'No, it's not. Everyone gets bitten by mosquitoes. There are lots here.'

'Yes, but mosquitoes don't do this to you.'

'Do what?' asked Ruby.

'Some were strange mosquitoes,' Alistair went on. 'Big ones. I have one – I squashed it. Do you want to see?'

'Not now, Alistair,' Ruby whispered, reaching out towards him.

'Let him speak,' the man said. 'Did you keep the mosquito you squashed?'

'Yes, it's in my book. Do you want to see?' he asked again.

'I think that might be a good idea. Why did you keep it?'

'I like things like that. Things that are unusual. I know about insects. I can remember science things.'

'Good lad. Me too.' The man smiled, a slightly crooked smile that didn't show his teeth. 'May I see your mosquito sample?'

Ruby was impressed at how he treated Alistair

– not as a freak, like everyone else did. That word, 'sample' – he was taking it seriously, treating Alistair like a scientist. She warmed to him, whoever he was.

'I wasn't bitten,' said Ava suddenly. 'Nathan was. But I wasn't. So I didn't fall ill.'

'Why weren't you bitten?'

'Mosquito repellant. I hate mosquitoes so I always use repellant.'

'Sounds like it was a good idea on this occasion.' The man took Ruby's arm and looked at some of the mosquito bites.

'Who are you?' she asked.

'Forgive me – how rude. I am Ignace; my other names – vary.'

'Do you live around here?'

'You could say that. And you?'

'I'm Ruby and this is my brother Alistair. Omar, Finn. And Ava. I see you've met Juliette already.' Juliette had not spoken for the whole time.

'Do you have any idea what has happened to you?' Ignace asked.

Ruby shook her head.

'Then this will come as a bit of a shock, I'm afraid. You might find it difficult to believe. You seem – though I don't really understand how this can have happened – to have been exposed to ... a virus. You have become vampires. Don't say anything. I know, it sounds impossible.'

'Yeah, right,' said Finn. 'Pull the other one. There's no such thing as vampires. This place is just crawling with nutters! First her, and now you!'

'I know it must seem like that. But look at the evidence. You don't appear to be breathing; you don't want to eat anything, except *her*. You only want to eat her, incidentally, because you can tell she's not one of us. She's a *blood*, and you can smell it.'

Ava looked horrified, shook her head.

'Excuse me, I know it's not polite. We would never normally call you that to your face. Bloods are very attractive to our kind. It is a struggle to resist the urge. But it must be resisted. You must learn how. It is my job to teach you how.'

'You're a nutcase. You think we're going to take vampire lessons from some creep who wanders around a Hungarian forest?'

'It's cool!' said Alistair. 'Can we fly and turn into bats and that?'

'Don't be stupid!' snapped Finn. 'That stuff's not real. Of course you're not a vampire.'

'No, you can't fly or turn into a bat. That's just in the movies. You will get the urge to suck blood from people and you must subdue it at all costs. You can eat bloody meat or take special capsules. You must not bite human beings. That passes on vampirism which is not cool, by the way – it is a curse, a terrible curse.'

'It doesn't sound too bad,' pondered Omar. 'Live forever, can't die except by staking. Plenty of time to achieve your ambitions.'

'Have you really thought about living forever?' asked Ignace. 'Living after all your family and friends are dead? Watching the world change around you until it is unrecognisable? You can't begin to understand the meaning of 'lonely' until you have lost everyone you ever loved. Finding new people to love every generation, and losing them again, and again, and again.'

'You want us to feel *sorry* for you?' Ruby couldn't believe it. 'You – if you really are a vampire – you destroy people, turn *them* into vampires. If it's so awful, why would you inflict it on anyone else?'

'Hunger. And loneliness. Vampires used to prey on those they loved to keep them, to drag them into eternity, because they couldn't bear to lose them. It doesn't happen now. We have rules.'

'Oh, so you've become all wishy-washy and compassionate? Huh.' Finn flicked a fly off his arm. 'Look, I'm even talking as though you exist. It's all rubbish!'

'Not compassionate. It's self-preservation. There were purges and hundreds of vampires were destroyed. Now we're careful. It's good that no one believes in us any more. We keep a low profile and so we survive. There are no bands of vampire hunters staking us, cutting our heads off, driving us out of our spaces. If you have truly become vampires – and I believe you have – you'll need to learn our ways.'

'We've just spent seventeen years being told

what to do by our parents and teachers and we're done with it. We aren't taking it from you and your kind, whoever or whatever you are,' said Omar.

'Fine. I'll leave you to tent-peg girl, then. Solves my problem.'

Ignace picked up Ava's bag of tent pegs and tossed it to her.

'Feel free. Oh, and get it right this time.'

Seven

'Wait!' Ava shouted. 'Don't leave me to them.'

'Afraid, my dear?' Ignace smiled properly, and they saw his fangs for the first time.

The sky darkened with the threat of a storm and long, hard drops of rain drummed on the leaves and pitted the sand of the shore. Ruby, Alistair, Finn and Omar crowded into the nearest tent. Ignace told Juliette and Ava to follow them.

He swore to Ava that he would be in the adjoining tent, keeping her safe.

The wind thrashed the tent flap so that it slapped to and fro, a dark triangle beating against the flysheet like a great wing. Juliette reached out to grab it, to zip it up, feeling the rain cold against her arm. Suddenly, strong fingers gripped her wrist.

Juliette screamed, trying to pull her arm free, but the fingers dug in tighter, hurting her, then twisting as though trying to break her arm.

'Help!' she managed to whimper through the pain. 'Something is holding me! Help!'

Before the others could do anything a shape blocked the entrance to the tent. The fabric made the shape indistinct. Blue jeans, white shirt, streaks of red. Juliette was still whimpering, tugging her arm to try to free it, but struggling made the grip tighter, the twisting more painful.

'Let me in.'

Ava gasped, scrabbled towards the back of the tent and tried to hide herself under sleeping bags.

'What are you doing?' shouted Omar, as she crawled over him. He lunged towards Juliette, grabbing her. The figure outside crouched down, not letting go of her wrist, and ripped the flap aside. His chest was covered with blood, spreading from the tent peg still sticking between the ribs.

'Little pigs, little pigs, let me come in,' he grinned, finally letting go of Juliette's wrist so that she fell backwards into Omar. His eyes scanned the tent, his face tight with fury and pain, until they fell on Ava cowering at the back. He lunged at her.

'You're supposed to be dead!' she wailed over the sleeping bag clutched in front of her.

'You wish!' he snarled.

Finn snatched the man's arm.

'Leave it! You aren't having your fight in here. If you two want to tear into each other, you can do it outside – tent-peg boy.'

The newcomer snarled, showing his teeth, but Finn didn't flinch.

'I'm not scared of you,' he said. 'I don't reckon you're up to much of a fight with that tent peg stuck in you – and I'm telling you, boy, I can fight.'

Nathan lunged towards Finn's neck, his mouth

open, threatening to bite.

'No, Nathan,' Ava shouted from the back of the tent. 'That won't work with him. You've picked the wrong fight this time.'

Finn and Nathan were still locked together, gripping each other's arms, head to head.

'So. You, too?' Omar said, as calmly as possible. 'I don't think fighting is the way forward. This is going to be difficult enough as it is.'

He laid a hand gently on Nathan's shoulder. 'Come on. Let's do the flaps up to keep the rain out and then talk.'

'I don't want to talk to you,' snarled Nathan. 'I want to get *her*.'

'Well, that's not going to happen. There are six

of us and one of you, and you aren't going to touch her. So can we have a civilised conversation?'

Nathan strained towards Finn, but wasn't strong enough to break his hold.

'She tried to kill me!'

'You tried to kill her. So can't you just say you're even?' Omar struggled to keep his temper.

'What about this?' Nathan pointed at the tent peg.

'Ah, that. It hadn't occurred to you to take it out?'

'You're not supposed to take out something you're impaled on,' said Alistair. 'It can cause more damage coming out than going in.'

'Shut up, math-boy,' snapped Finn.

'Look, we're all in this together, whether we like

it or not,' said Juliette at last.

'You shut up, too, vamp-tramp.'

Juliette turned on Finn in fury, but Omar caught her arm.

'Stop it, everyone!'

The flaps of the tent parted. It was Ignace.

'You're not doing very well, are you?'

'And who are you?' shouted Nathan. 'I'm going to kill that – '

'No, you're not. For one thing, if you bite her you won't kill her – you'll just be stuck with her for eternity. I don't want to be policing you lot for the next 400 years any more than you want me to be doing it. But this has happened on my patch, and I'm going to sort it out – at least for tonight. You – Nathan, is it? – outside. I can remove that tent peg safely.'

Nathan didn't move. He scowled at Ignace.

'Now. Do it.'

Nathan backed out of the tent and sat, sullen, at Ignace's feet.

'We need some flour,' Ignace continued. 'Do you have any?'

'No,' said Ruby. 'Why would we?'

'Bread?'

'Stale bread any good?' She handed him the food bag out of the tent.

Ignace made Nathan lie on the ground, despite

the rain which pounded against his wet shirt.

'This will hurt,' he said as he took hold of the end of the tent peg. 'Bite on some bread and try not to scream – we don't want to attract attention if anyone is around. Ava, get out here.'

When Ava was beside him, shivering and soon drenched, Ignace hauled on the tent peg, drawing it slowly from Nathan's chest.

As he pulled, Nathan's back arched and he growled in agony through the bread clenched between his teeth. Ava felt sick.

As the tent peg came out, red along its length, a little blood pooled on Nathan's chest and Ignace immediately dropped bread onto the wound. The bread soaked it up from beneath, turning into a deep red sop. For a moment, Ava remembered the bread-and-milk sop her grandmother used to make for her when she was ill as a child.

'Now, you, open your mouth,' commanded Ignace. And though Ava opened it to object, Ignace stuffed the blood-sop between her lips and then closed her mouth with his hand.

'Eat it.'

She struggled desperately to spit it out, the metallic, salty tang of the blood making her feel as sick as the idea of it. She tried to open her mouth, tried to cry 'Can't' and 'No', but his hand covered her nose and mouth and she couldn't breathe unless she swallowed it.

Eight

Nathan rolled onto his side, clutching his chest.

Finn launched himself from the tent at Ignace's legs, but the man took no notice, brushing him off as though he were a fly.

'You're a total freak! What was all that about?'

'Immunity. I thought you knew all about vampires? To cure someone bitten by a vampire, they have to eat bread made from flour and the vampire's own blood. You didn't have flour. This will do. The bread is just a way of getting the blood in.'

Ava, free to breathe again, was gasping and retching.

'Don't sick it up – we'll just have to do it again,' Ignace said sternly. Ava was white, holding her throat, with either rain or tears streaming down her face. Or perhaps both.

'But he didn't bite her, she said he didn't. Even if this were all true, he didn't bite her,' yelled Finn.

'It's like a vaccination,' Ignace said, calm as ever. 'Protection against the virus. She'll be immune to vampire bites within a matter of hours. Then you won't need to control your teenage-boy urges. Which is just as well, as you don't seem to be very good at that.'

'Nor you your old-man urges. You're old enough to be Juliette's father – in fact, her great-great-great-great-great-grandfather if we're to believe you. What's going on there?'

Omar had appeared at the tent opening. But he stopped at the sight of the blood around Ava's mouth. 'And what's going on here?'

'I just explained – vaccination. Vampirism is caused by a virus.'

'But you made her eat his blood? That's gross!'

'And creepy,' added Ruby. 'Does it work?'

'Yes. If any of you – or a mosquito – bites her, she will be protected against vampirism. But you won't feel the desire to bite her. Mosquitoes will, of course, but they can't harm her now.'

'How long does it last?' asked Ruby.

'Forever, as far as I know. That is, as long as she lives. Because she will die in seventy or eighty years, of course. And you won't. That will take some getting used to.'

It would indeed. They were all silent, even Finn, for a long time.

'So,' Omar said at last. 'Do we have a choice?'

'Die now or live forever? Too late – the choice has been made for you. You live forever – virtually. Nathan, you're lucky she got it wrong – you nearly got the other option. Now – we need to talk. There's a lot to learn.'

Vampire Dawn

The story starts with **Die Now or Live Forever**. Read it first.

Then follow each individual's story. You can read these in any order:

Juliette's story

Finn's story

Omar's story

Alistair and Ruby's story

Ava's story

Plus an essential guide for new vampires.

Find out more at www.vampiredawn.co.uk. Follow the vampires on Facebook: www.facebook.com/VampireDawnBooks
twitter: @vampiredawn